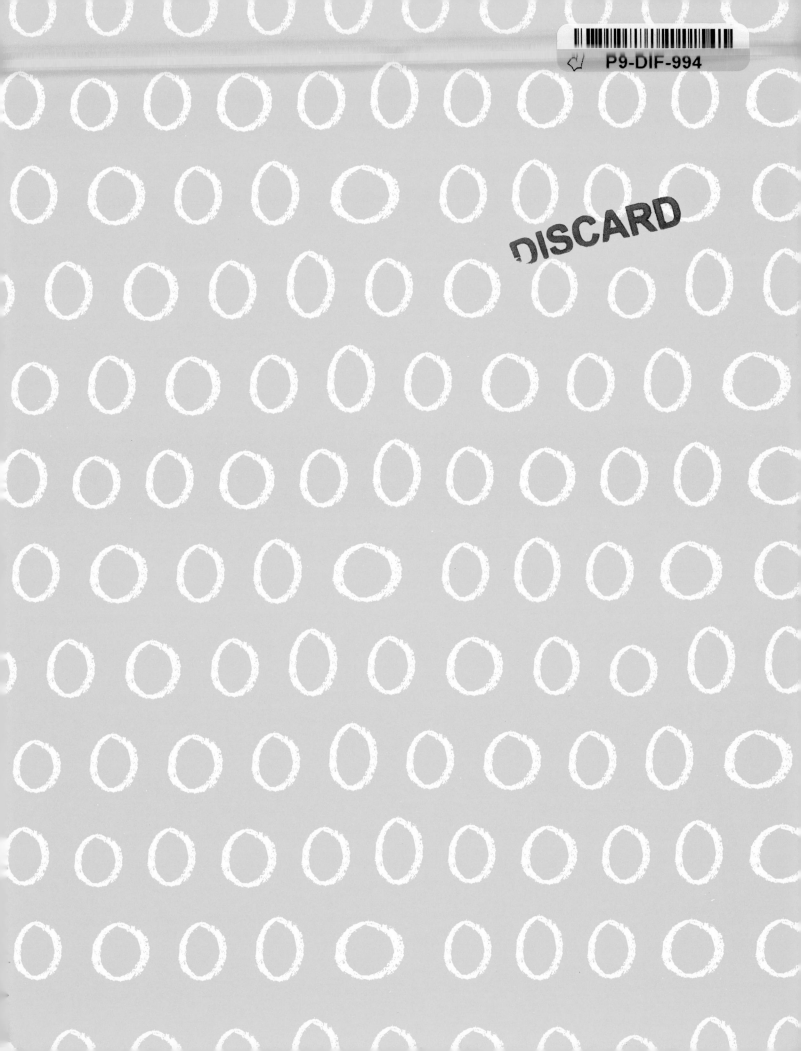

Octopus Stew

ERIC VELASQUEZ

HOLIDAY HOUSE • NEW YORK

When Grandma saw my painting of Super Octo, she got the idea to make pulpo guisado, octopus stew—not exactly my favorite dish.

"But Dad makes that," I said.

Grandma snapped at me, "I've been making pulpo guisado since your dad era un niño, since he was a boy."

I didn't want to upset her, so I didn't ask any more questions.

So later, while I was playing Super Ram
with Chana, Grandma told me to get ready
to go shopping with her.

Grandma gave me a look and said, "¿Qué es esto?
Boy, if you think I am going to
the store with you wearing
that silly cape, you've
lost your mind."

At the store I saw lots of cool-looking fish. I took pictures so I could look them up later on.

Grandma picked the biggest octopus in the store. She said it was the best of the bunch. It looked like it was still alive to me . . . and kind of creepy.

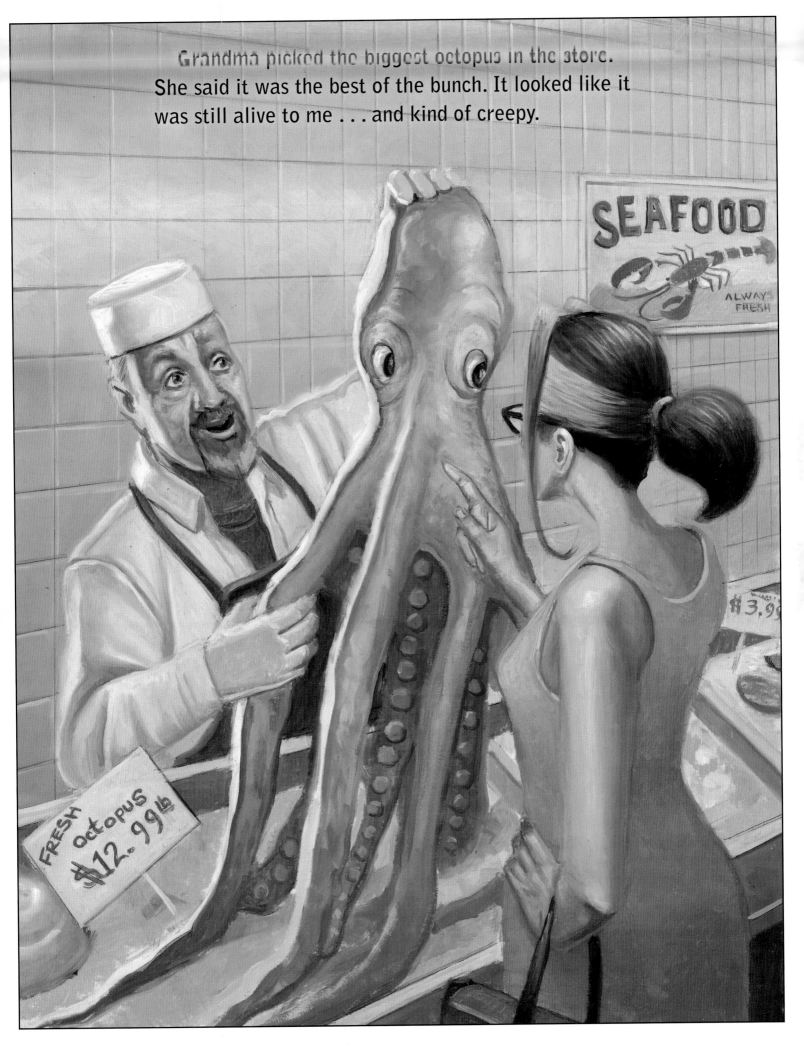

I decided to do some
web surfing when a warning
popped up on my screen
about octopuses.

I tried to tell Grandma, but she wouldn't let me. "How often do I have to tell you to keep that thing in your pocket when you go out with me!" she said.

Back home, Grandma unwrapped the octopus, gave it
a good scrubbing, and put it in a pot of boiling water.
I did my best to stay out of her way.

Then Grandma came to sit with me while I did my homework. All of a sudden, strange noises started to come from the kitchen.

Blimp, Blump, Brr, Blimp, Blump, Brrr.

"¿Que será eso? What could that be?" Grandma asked. "Ramsey, quédate aquí. Voy a ver. Stay here. "

The sounds got louder.
Bloop, Bloop, Bloop, Brrrr. Bloop, Bloop, Bloop, Brrrr.

The octopus got so big it blew
the lid off the pot.

"¡Wela, tenga cuidado!
Grandma, watch out!" I warned.
"Escóndete!" Grandma
hollered. "Hide!"

Thump!

Thump!

BRRRR!

Thump!

bloop

Thump!

blop

"¡Vámonos de aquí!" I yelled.
"Let's get out of here!"

But it was too late.

I grabbed my phone and hid until I could figure out how to rescue Grandma.

The octopus had to have a natural predator, something that it feared. I searched, and there it was: Sharks!

I grabbed my drawing pad and markers and drew the
biggest, meanest, scariest shark I could create.

I put on my Super Ram cape and marched into the kitchen.

"You put down my grandma," I yelled.

Dad interrupted. "Okay mijo, don't you think this is getting a little far-fetched? I mean like, really, Ramsey?"

The octopus dropped Grandma
and attacked, spraying ink all over
my drawing.

"Hey, Dad, you broke my concentration! It's my turn
to tell the story tonight. May I please finish now?"

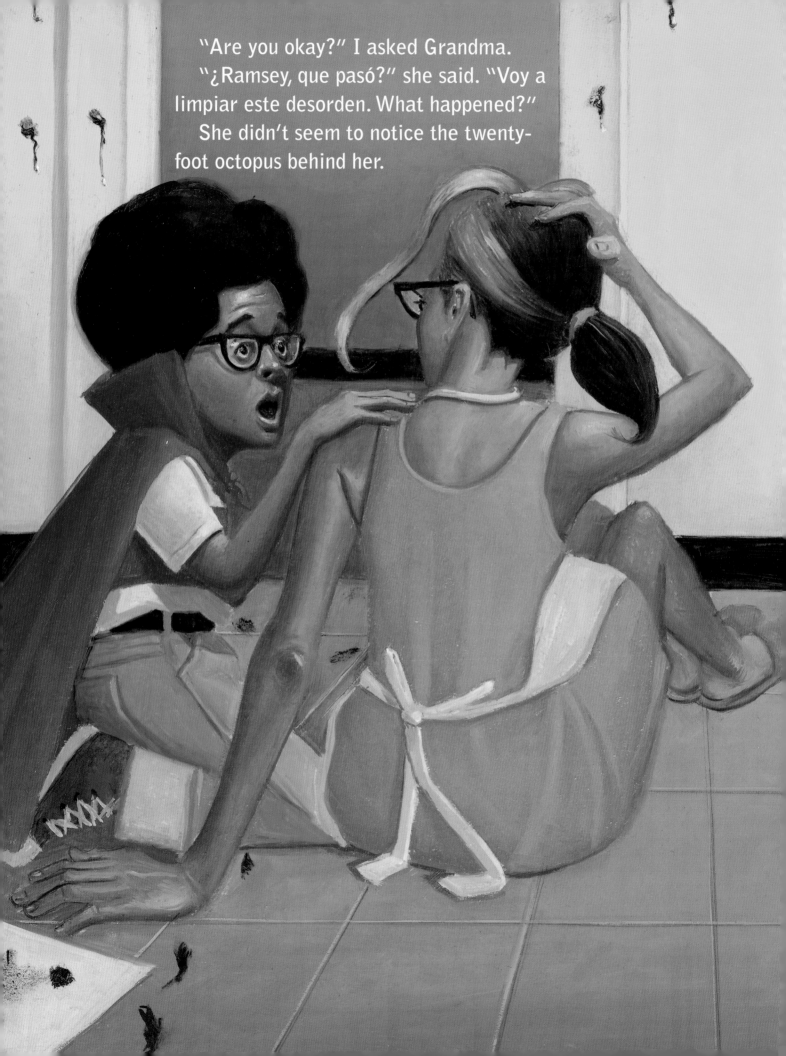

Then I remembered the warning that popped up on my phone and read it out loud. "Important, before cooking an octopus remove the eyes and beak . . ."

"Basta ya. That's enough, Señor Pulpo," said Grandma. "I changed my mind. We are no longer having pulpo guisado. Instead we are having ensalada sin pulpo. Just salad, no octopus."

And Señor Pulpo joined us.

When I was young, my family would often gather together and enjoy food, music, dance, and stories. It was a wonderful time; we children were also encouraged to tell stories, play an instrument, sing, or dance. The story of the octopus is still a family favorite, often told by my dad, who actually rescued my grandma and me from an overflowing octopus.

With this version of the story I also wanted to share with the reader the sense of pride Ramsey's family has in being Afro-Latino, embracing their African heritage from the ancient tradition of oral storytelling to their love of art and cooking.

I loved comic books and the TV shows *Adventures of Superman* and *Batman*. When I was visiting Grandma, she would allow me to wear my Superman-inspired cape (recycled from an old Halloween costume) all year round with the understanding that if someone knocked on the door or if we were going out, I would have to take it off.

I named the character Ramsey because I once asked my mom if she had not named me Eric what would my name have been. She mentioned several names including Kwame, after Kwame Nkrumah who, around the time of my birth, was responsible for Ghana's independence, and Ramsey, because the name was derived from Ramses, the Egyptian pharaoh.

My mom decided to name me Eric after a high school English teacher she had in Puerto Rico, who introduced the class to the English language and helped inspire my mom's lifelong love of reading.

Please note that my family spoke non-standard Spanish at home, which is reflected in this book.

Wela	my name for my grandma	WEH-lah
pulpo guisado	octopus stew	POOL-poh ghee-SOW
era un niño	was a boy	EH-rah oon NEEN-yoh
Chana	our dog's name	CHAH-nah
¿Qué es esto?	What is this?	keh ehs ES-toh
¿Que será eso?	What could that be?	keh se-RAH EH-so
Quedate aqui. Voy a ver.	Stay here. I'm going to look.	KEH-dah-teh ah-KEE. Voy ah vair.
¡Wela, tenga cuidado!	Grandma, be careful!	WEH-lah, TEN-ghah kwee-DAH-toh
Escondete!	Hide!	Es-COHN-deh-te
¡Vámonos de aquí!	Let's get out of here!	VAH-moh-nohs deh ah-KEE
mijo	son	MEE-hoh
¿Que pasó?	What happened?	keh pah-SOH
Voy a limpiar este desorden.	I'm going to clean this mess	voy ah LEEM-pee-AHL EH-steh deh-SOR-dehn
Basta ya.	That's enough.	BAH-stah yah
Señor Pulpo	Mr. Octopus	sehn-YOR POOL-poh
ensalada sin pulpo	salad without octopus	ehn-sah-LAH-dah seen POOL-poh

Octopus Stew Recipe

You can make Octopus Stew too, with Eric's dad's recipe. Be sure to get an adult to help you!

INGREDIENTS:

1 octopus, approximately 4 pounds
1 lemon
vinegar
1 bay leaf
½ tablespoon of oregano
½ teaspoon of Himalayan pink salt (or to taste)
olive oil to coat the bottom of the sauce pot
1 medium onion, chopped
½ green pepper, chopped

4 garlic cloves, crushed or diced
1 roasted red pepper, sliced small
½ cup of stuffed green olives, whole or sliced in half
½ teaspoon of Himalayan pink salt (or to taste)
½ teaspoon of black pepper (or to taste)
1 8-oz can of tomato sauce
1 cup of water
1 teaspoon of white vinegar
cilantro to taste

Cut the lemon in half and gently scrub the octopus, rinsing under running water. Remove the eyes and beak and rinse with water and vinegar. Rinse and clean inside of sac. (Most frozen octopus have the inside of the sac already removed.)

Combine the bay leaf, oregano, and salt in a pot of water and bring it to a boil. The octopus can be added to the water just as it is beginning to boil. Boil the octopus for approximately 1½ hours or until tender.

In a medium sauce pot, heat the olive oil and sauté the onion, green pepper, and garlic. Once onions are translucent, add the red pepper. While gently stirring, add the tomato sauce and a cup of water, salt and black pepper, cilantro, olives, and the white vinegar. Let simmer.

Drain the octopus and let it cool slightly. The skin should be purple and easily slide off, revealing a pinkish-white meat.

On a cutting board, slice the octopus into small circular pieces. Add to the sauce and let simmer for 30 to 40 minutes, stirring occasionally.

Serve over white rice or with boiled green bananas.

Enjoy!

For my dad, my first storytelling mentor, and for all those young storytellers who continue in the tradition of sharing and telling stories.

Copyright © 2019 by Eric Velasquez
All Rights Reserved
HOLIDAY HOUSE is registered in the U.S. Patent and Trademark Office.
Printed and bound in May 2019 at Toppan Leefung, DongGuan City, China.
The illustrations were painted in oil on Fabriano 300 lb. hot press watercolor paper.
www.holidayhouse.com
First Edition
1 3 5 7 9 10 8 6 4 2

Library of Congress Cataloging-in-Publication Data

Names: Velasquez, Eric, author, illustrator.
Title: Octopus stew / Eric Velasquez.
Description: First edition. | New York : Holiday House, [2019] | Summary: Ramsey dons his superhero cape to rescue Grandma from the huge octopus she is trying to cook—or is he simply telling a story? Includes author's note on the story's origin and a recipe for Octopus stew.
Identifiers: LCCN 2019013411 | ISBN 9780823437542 (hardback)
Subjects: | CYAC: Grandmothers—Fiction. | Octopuses—Fiction. | Cooking—Fiction. | Storytelling—Fiction. | Hispanic Americans—Fiction. | African Americans—Fiction. | Humorous stories. | BISAC: JUVENILE FICTION / Family / Multigenerational. | JUVENILE FICTION / People & Places / United States / African American. | JUVENILE FICTION / Cooking & Food.
Classification: LCC PZ7.V4878 Oct 2019 | DDC [E]--dc23
LC record available at https://lccn.loc.gov/2019013411

ISBN: 978-0-8234-3754-2 (hardcover)